The Backward Easter Egg Hunt

Meadow Rue Merrill

 HENDRICKSON PUBLISHERS ROSE KiDZ

Lantern Hill Farm: The Backward Easter Egg Hunt

RoseKidz® is an imprint of
Rose Publishing, LLC
P.O. Box 3473
Peabody, Massachusetts 01961-3473 USA
www.hendricksonrose.com

Cover Design by Drew Krevi
Illustrations by Drew Krevi
Book Production by Drew McCall

ISBN: 978-1-62862-795-4
RoseKidz® reorder #L50027
JUVENILE FICTION / Religious / Christian / Holidays & Celebrations

Printed in China

Printed September 2018

To _Sam_

From _Easter Bunny_

Date _4/12/2020_

For Jenny and Gerry, who shine.

*When anyone lives in Christ, the new creation
has come. The old is gone! The new is here!*

2 Corinthians 5:17

Molly peeked at the calendar.
Only three days 'til Easter!

Easter was a sparkly new dress. Easter was baby chicks and fuzzy lambs. Best of all, Easter was a giant Easter egg hunt at Lantern Hill Farm.

Each spring, Aunt Jenny filled hollow eggs with treats and hid them in the barn.

Neighbors came for a huge picnic. Then the children raced to find the eggs.

Molly couldn't wait! She twirled down the hall to find her Easter basket.

On Easter morning, Molly was the first one dressed. She was first in the car. And first in church. Even Baby Charlie wanted to hurry. When the pastor said, "Amen," Baby Charlie made a loud, "Whoop!"

6

"How long 'til the Easter egg hunt?" Molly asked on the way to the farm.

"Aunt Jenny is planning something different this year," said Mama.

"It's a surprise," said Papa.

The only surprise Molly wanted was how many eggs would fit in her basket.

At the farm, Uncle Gerry held a newborn lamb.

"Is this your surprise?" asked Molly.

Aunt Jenny smiled like she was hiding a secret.
"Wait until after lunch. Then you'll see."

Molly didn't want to wait.

She peeked in the barn. No eggs!

She peeked under a bucket. No eggs!

She peeked behind a barrel. Just a fluffy yellow chick.

Where had Aunt Jenny hidden all the eggs?

9

10

Molly's cousin Jacob and his little brother, Sammy, burst into the barn.

"Time to eat!" said Jacob.

"Where are the Easter eggs?" asked Molly.

"That's part of the surprise," said Sammy.

11

More friends and neighbors began to show up at Lantern Hill Farm. Molly saw her friend Rosa and Rosa's mother. Rosa was wearing a pretty yellow dress.

Molly sat with her Papa and Mama and Baby Charlie for the picnic. Then she saw something. Eggs! A whole basketful of eggs were on the farmhouse porch.

"Aunt Jenny forgot to hide the eggs!" Molly gasped.

"Are you surprised?" asked Papa.

Molly frowned. This was not the surprise she'd been expecting.

12

"Time for the
Easter egg hunt!"
Aunt Jenny called.

Molly pointed.
"I already found them."

Aunt Jenny laughed. "Instead of hiding eggs,
this year I am giving you empty eggs to fill."

"That's backward!" said Molly.

14

"A backward Easter egg hunt!" Sammy clapped. "Are you surprised?"

Molly was surprised Aunt Jenny thought this was a good idea. "What are we supposed to find?" she asked.

"Things to remind us of parts of the Easter story," Aunt Jenny said as she handed each child a list.

Something prickly
Something red
Something living
Something already dead
Something heavy
Something light
Something dark
Something bright

"Pick a partner," Aunt Jenny said as Uncle Gerry handed out eggs. Molly and Sammy looked at each other and nodded. They'd be partners! "When you find something on your list, put it inside an egg. When you've found everything on the list, race back to me. Ready? Set? Go!"

18

"Something prickly?"
asked Sammy.

"Hay!" Molly and
Sammy raced
toward the barn.

"Something red?" asked Molly.

"A berry!" They zipped
toward the garden.

After filling their eggs, Molly
and Sammy sprinted back.

19

"Well done!" Aunt Jenny handed them a prize.

Molly and Sammy clapped as each team finished the race.

Then Aunt Jenny gathered the children. "What is prickly?"

"A twig!" said Rosa.

"A pine needle!" said a boy.

"A porcupine quill!" said Jacob.

21

"How are they part of the Easter story?" asked Aunt Jenny. "Remember: prickly things hurt."

Molly remembered what the pastor had said in church.

"The nails that held Jesus to the cross hurt. So did the crown of thorns they put on his head," Molly said.

"Right," Aunt Jenny said. "Jesus healed people who were sick. He fed people who were hungry. He forgave people who did wrong. But he was hurt anyway."

23

"What is red?" Aunt Jenny continued.

The children held up a red flower, a red button, and Sammy's red strawberry.

"When Jesus was hurt, his blood was red," said Aunt Jenny. "It shows how much he loved us. What did you find that is living?"

"A leaf." Molly opened her egg.

"My leaf is already dead," said Jacob.

"Jesus died, too." Aunt Jenny looked sad. "He gave his life for you and me. But death is not the end. Who found something heavy?"

Sammy held up a rock.

Aunt Jenny nodded. "After Jesus died, his body was placed in a tomb. A heavy stone closed the door. Three days later, God rolled away the stone. To God it was as light as—"

"A feather!" Molly opened her egg,
and a feather floated out.

Aunt Jenny nodded. "Nothing is stronger than God,"
she said. "Not a rock. Not even death. Jesus is alive!
It was a miracle—something only God can do."

27

"Why something dark?" Sammy emptied dirt from his egg.

"When we lie. Or say mean words. Or hurt people, all the light inside us goes dark," said Aunt Jenny.

"But God forgives us, right?" asked Jacob.

"Yes." Aunt Jenny smiled. "God sent Jesus to take away our darkness. When we pray and ask God to forgive us, he fills us with light. Then we become all bright and sparkly inside, like—"

"Did you like Aunt Jenny's surprise?" Papa asked on the way home.

"Yes!" Molly grinned. "Can we do a backward Easter egg hunt next year? Then I can help Baby Charlie find things that remind us of the Easter story!"

Mama smiled. Papa parked the car, and Molly hopped up the steps to count the days 'til next Easter.

Not just because
she'd get to wear a
sparkly new dress.

Or because of baby
chicks and fuzzy lambs.

Or because of
Aunt Jenny's giant
Easter egg hunt.

But because Easter meant celebrating
God's great love—the kind that makes
you brand-new and sparkly, too.

31

To hold your own backward Easter egg hunt, invite your friends and neighbors. Use the scavenger list from this story, or create your own based on the Easter story found in Luke 23 and 24. All you need is a basket of plastic eggs, a bunch of kids, and your imagination.

For more from Meadow Rue Merrill, including other exciting ideas for celebrating God's love, visit her page on HendricksonRose.com.